DANIEL'S TRAIN

A Red Fox Book

Published by Random House Children's Books
20 Vauxhall Bridge Road, London SW1V 2SA

A division of Random House UK Ltd
London Melbourne Sydney Auckland
Johannesburg and agencies throughout the world

1 3 5 7 9 10 8 6 4 2

First published in Great Britain by Hutchinson Children's Books 1995

Red Fox edition 1999

Printed in Singapore

RANDOM HOUSE UK Limited Reg. No. 954009

ISBN 0 091 87292 8

DANIEL'S TRAIN

Illustrations and story line Allan Curless
Text Angela McAllister

RED FOX

The train pulled into the station. The boy, Daniel, did not want to get off.
He was dreaming of travelling on with Bear; on and on to the end of the line.
'Hurry up, Dan,' said his mother. 'We'll miss our stop.'

Daniel followed his mother on to the platform. Then he stopped, startled by a noise. Was someone calling his name? No, when he turned round, the platform was empty.

Back at home, Daniel made tracks through the country of his room.

'It feels like Bear's bedtime,' he said. But Bear was not there.

'Don't worry,' said his mother. 'All bears like stories and a warm bed. He will soon turn up.'

But Bear did not turn up. He did not climb into Daniel's bed that night.

Bear did not come home the next day either.

'He's gone without me,' said Daniel to himself. 'All the way to the end of the line.'

In the afternoon, he asked Mum to take him to the railway museum. He wandered around until he found exactly what he was looking for – a small green engine with a whistle and a funnel.

The cab door was open and Daniel climbed inside. He put on the driver's big gloves, pulled the whistle and closed his eyes.

Suddenly, the engine gave a jolt! A fire started to crackle in the furnace and steam began to hiss from the pipes.

Fizzle-crack! The train started to move; and slowly and heavily it chugged into a dark tunnel.

Daniel's train gained speed. Faster and faster, it roared into the darkness and then shot out over the rooftops through billows of steam. On and on, and up and up, it rattled over the chimneypots. Sparks and soot filled the air with the smell of fire.

'On and up!' cried Daniel, the driver.

The train hurtled into a starry sky. Daniel took hold of the silver wheel. He pulled the whistle and stoked the furnace until the little green engine was flying as fast as a comet. They wound through the twilight and into the night. Then, higher and higher, across the great bridge of time, back into day and down into a forest.

The forest creatures came out of hiding to watch Daniel's train.

'Where is the end of the line?' called Daniel.

'On and on,' replied the animals.

Before long, the little green engine began to slow down. Without knowing why, Daniel knew he had reached his journey's end. The country had changed; but it was strangely familiar.

A signal box appeared, then a station.

Daniel pulled the brake and climbed down.

'I've come for Bear,' he said to the stationmaster. 'Medium sized, brown, quite scruffy…and probably very tired.'

'Well,' replied the stationmaster. 'He is certainly here. We have dolls, and jack-in-the-boxes, monkeys and soldiers…and we have bears of all kinds.'

'I'm sure I've seen your bear,' said a jack-in-the-box. 'He has one eye and a red ribbon.'

'No, that's not Bear,' said Daniel.

'I know your teddy,' said a clown. 'He's awfully fat and is wearing a blue jumper.'

'Bear is not fat at all!' said Daniel.

'Come with us,' said a doll. 'We'll show you where the bears live.'

Daniel met bears of all kinds. Brown and red and yellow; big and small and medium sized; growling bears and musical bears.

But not his bear.

Daniel returned to the station.

'I'm sorry you didn't find your bear,' said the stationmaster. 'But this train is ready to go.' He waved his red flag and cried, 'All aboard!'

Sadly, Daniel climbed into the engine. Only the setting sun noticed a small passenger slip out of the waiting room.

The train rolled slowly down
the track. As Daniel reached
for the driver's gloves he felt a
paw slip into his hand.

Bear gave Daniel a sorry look.

'I know,' said Daniel. 'Sometimes
a bear likes an adventure.'

'But mostly,' replied Bear,
'he likes stories and a warm bed.'

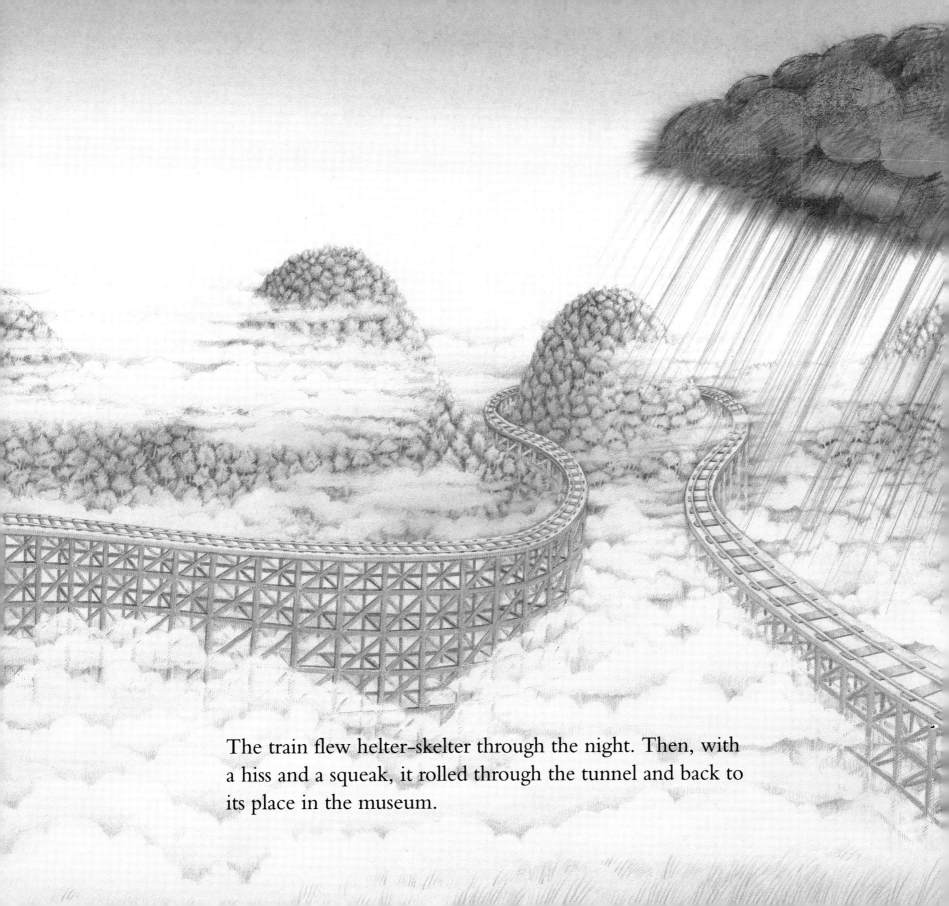

The train flew helter-skelter through the night. Then, with a hiss and a squeak, it rolled through the tunnel and back to its place in the museum.

Daniel's mother was waiting to lift him down.

'Where have you been in your old green engine?' she asked.

'All the way to the end of the line,' said Daniel.

'And did you find what you were looking for?' said his mother.

Daniel didn't answer, but just held very tightly on to Bear's paw.